CELEBRATING JUNETEENTH

BY JODY JENSEN SHAFFER · ILLUSTRATED BY KATHLEEN PETELINSEK

The **Child's World®**
childsworld.com

Published by The Child's World®
1980 Lookout Drive • Mankato, MN 56003-1705
800-599-READ • www.childsworld.com

ISBN 9781503853898 (Reinforced Library Binding)
ISBN 9781503854697 (Portable Document Format)
ISBN 9781503855076 (Online Multi-user eBook)
LCCN: 2021953053

Printed in the United States of America

ABOUT THE AUTHOR

Jody Jensen Shaffer is the author
of dozens books for children.
She also publishes poetry,
stories, and articles in children's
magazines. Jody works from
her home in Missouri.

ABOUT THE ILLUSTRATOR

Kathleen Petelinsek is a
freelance illustrator in the
Minneapolis area.
She has loved to draw
since childhood.

CONTENTS

CHAPTER 1

Let's Celebrate!

It's June 19. People are outside. They are having fun! They dance. They eat BBQ. They drink strawberry pop. Kids play games. People listen to speeches. What are they celebrating? It's Juneteenth! A day that **commemorates** the end of slavery in the United States.

People celebrating Juneteenth.

CHAPTER 2

What was Slavery?

In the 1600s and 1700s, Black people were stolen from their homes in Africa. They were brought to the American colonies and **enslaved**. They were forced to work without pay. They worked in fields. They worked in homes. Enslavers split up Black families. They treated them badly.

In the northern United States, enslaved people often worked in cities. In the south, most enslaved people worked on large farms called **plantations**.

Some people were against enslaving people. They thought slavery was wrong. In 1808, Congress stepped in. It said enslaved people could no longer be brought into the country. But slavery continued in the south. Enslavers there claimed they needed the labor of the unpaid workers.

People were sold as property. Families were split apart. Parents and children were separated.

A Civil War started in 1861 over slavery.

By 1860, there were nearly 4 million enslaved people in the U.S. Many people in the north wanted to end slavery. Most people in the south did not.

The fight over slavery grew. In 1860, Abraham Lincoln was elected president. He was against slavery. He wanted to make it against the law.

This started a war in 1861. It was called the Civil War. States in the north were part of the **Union**. They did not want slavery. States in the south were in the **Confederacy**. They wanted slavery to continue.

CHAPTER 3

You Are Free!

President Lincoln did not want anyone to be enslaved. On January 1, 1863 he signed the **Emancipation Proclamation**. It said all enslaved people in the Confederacy were free! But states in the Confederacy did not want to follow Lincoln's orders. Texas was part of the Confederacy. Around 250,000 people were enslaved there. Enslavers in Texas did not tell their workers they were free!

This map shows the Union and Confederate states during the Civil War.

KEY
- ■ Union States
- ■ Territories
- ■ Confederate States of America

President Lincoln signed the Emancipation Proclamation on January 1, 1863 to free enslaved people.

The enslaved people finally found out more than two years later. On June 19, 1865, General Gordon Granger rode into town. He led Union Army soldiers to Galveston, Texas. The soldiers went there to take back the state. They brought a special message from the president. You are free!

General Granger read Order Number 3. It said, "The people of Texas are informed that . . . all slaves are free."

People cheered! They prayed. They sang. They danced. Some left Texas right away. They went to find family in the north. They went where they were welcome.

In December of 1865, the 13th Amendment to the U.S. Constitution was passed. It said that slavery was against the law.

CHAPTER 4

Early Juneteenth Celebrations

People call Juneteenth different things. Some call it Jubilee Day. Some call it Freedom Day. Some call it Emancipation Day. The word Juneteenth comes from "June" and "nineteenth." It was the day all enslaved people were freed!

The first Juneteenth celebration took place in Texas in 1866. Freed men, women, and children gathered. They prayed and sang. They ate and marched. Some wore new clothes. The clothes stood for their new freedom. More communities joined in. Several groups bought land. This land was used to celebrate Juneteenth. They called the land Emancipation Park. The celebrations spread. People outside of Texas joined in. Many in the United States celebrated. Many in the world celebrated!

Early Juneteenth celebrations were often held at churches. Some were held in fields in the country.

Some of the first Juneteenth celebrations were held in churches. People dressed in new clothing and sang songs.

13

CHAPTER 5

A National Holiday

Juneteenth wasn't as popular in the 1960s. African Americans focused on other things. They fought hard for their **civil rights**. Dr. Martin Luther King Jr. was one of many people who led the fight. He wanted Black people to have the same rights as whites. He wanted Black people to be able to vote. He wanted them to have access to a good education. He wanted fair trials.

Dr. Martin Luther King Jr.

Opal Lee is a grandmother from Texas. Although in her 90s, she walked all across the country to bring attention to Juneteenth and the need for a national holiday.

Juneteenth... A NATIONAL HOLIDAY

Texas was the first state to make Juneteenth a holiday. In 1980, Al Edwards, an African American state legislator, introduced a bill that made it official.

Juneteenth became popular again in the 1970s. Texas made Juneteenth a state holiday in 1980. Some people wanted it to be a national holiday. When he was a senator, Barack Obama tried to make it a national holiday.

Juneteenth finally became a national holiday in 2021. Other countries also celebrate the day. They use it to mark the end of slavery. They celebrate the stories of African Americans. They honor all they have done.

CHAPTER 6

Juneteenth Celebrations

What happens on Juneteenth? Each city does it differently! Celebrations can be one day. They can be one week. They can even be one month long. People eat together. They eat red foods and drinks. Watermelon, strawberries, and red soda are good! Red is a **symbol** of freedom!

Storytelling is a big part of Juneteenth celebrations. Stories remind people about the first days of freedom.

Red food represents freedom.

Families play baseball on Juneteenth.

People go fishing. They play baseball. They listen to speeches. They learn about the past and dream about the future. They pray and sing. In some places, people put on plays. They act out the day General Granger rode to Texas. There are parades. Bands play music. Dancers dance. Museums hold events. Some companies give employees the day off. People register to vote.

CHAPTER 7

A Song Celebrating Juneteenth

James Weldon Johnson wrote a poem in 1900. It was called "Lift Ev'ry Voice and Sing." His brother J. Rosamond Johnson set it to music. Over the years, many people have sung this song. They sing it at Juneteenth celebrations. It is sometimes called the "Black National Anthem." In 2020, the National Football League played this song before each season opener game.

LIFT EVERY VOICE AND SING

Lift ev'ry voice and sing,
'Til earth and heaven ring,
Ring with the harmonies of Liberty;
Let our rejoicing rise
High as the list'ning skies,
Let it resound loud as the rolling sea.
Sing a song full of the faith that the dark past has taught us,
Sing a song full of the hope that the present has brought us;
Facing the rising sun of our new day begun,
Let us march on 'til victory is won.

Stony the road we trod,
Bitter the chastening rod,
Felt in the days when hope unborn had died;
Yet with a steady beat,
Have not our weary feet
Come to the place for which our fathers sighed?

We have come over a way that with tears has been watered,
We have come, treading our path through the blood
    of the slaughtered,
Out from the gloomy past,
'Til now we stand at last
Where the white gleam of our bright star is cast.

God of our weary years,
God of our silent tears,
Thou who has brought us thus far on the way;
Thou who has by Thy might
Led us into the light,
Keep us forever in the path, we pray.
Lest our feet stray from the places, our God, where we met Thee,
Lest, our hearts drunk with the wine of the world, we forget Thee;
Shadowed beneath Thy hand,
May we forever stand,
True to our God,
True to our native land.

Imagine the feeling if you were enslaved and you found out you were free.

21

CHAPTER 8

Poetry Corner

Frances Ellen Watkins Harper

Frances Ellen Watkins Harper was a teacher and **abolitionist**. She was against slavery. She was one of the first African American women to be published in the United States. "Bury Me in a Free Land" was published in her 1854 book *Poems on Miscellaneous Subjects*.

BURY ME IN A FREE LAND

Make me a grave where'er you will,
In a lowly plain, or a lofty hill;
Make it among earth's humblest graves,
But not in a land where men are slaves.
I could not rest if around my grave
I heard the steps of a trembling slave;
His shadow above my silent tomb
Would make it a place of fearful gloom.
I could not rest if I heard the tread
Of a coffle gang to the shambles led,
And the mother's shriek of wild despair
Rise like a curse on the trembling air.
I could not sleep if I saw the lash
Drinking her blood at each fearful gash,
And I saw her babes torn from her breast,

Like trembling doves from their parent nest.
I'd shudder and start if I heard the bay
Of bloodhounds seizing their human prey,
And I heard the captive plead in vain
As they bound afresh his galling chain.
If I saw young girls from their mother's arms
Bartered and sold for their youthful charms,
My eye would flash with a mournful flame,
My death-paled cheek grow red with shame.
I would sleep, dear friends, where bloated might
Can rob no man of his dearest right;
My rest shall be calm in any grave
Where none can call his brother a slave.
I ask no monument, proud and high,
To arrest the gaze of the passers-by;
All that my yearning spirit craves,
Is bury me not in a land of slaves.

JOINING IN THE SPIRIT OF JUNETEENTH

* Is there a Juneteenth celebration in your area? If so, go and enjoy the sights and sounds!

* What does it mean to be free? Write a poem or song about what freedom means to you.

* One of our greatest freedoms is the ability to choose our leaders. Ask the people in your family if they are registered to vote. If not, help them get registered.

MAKING A CELEBRATION FLAG

You can celebrate Juneteenth by creating your own flag. Flags are usually rectangular. They have colors and pictures that are meaningful. Take your flag with you to celebrate Juneteenth!

What you need:
Stiff cardboard (like cereal boxes)
Pieces of brightly colored paper
Glue stick
Scissors
Markers
Pencil

Directions
1. Draw an outline of your flag on the cardboard.
2. Cut it out.
3. Decide on your design and colors.
4. Cut and glue paper on the cardboard.
5. Use markers to make designs.

MAKING RED VELVET CAKE

What you need:

Cake:
1/2 cup shortening
1 1/2 cups white sugar
2 large eggs
2 tablespoons cocoa
4 tablespoons red food coloring
1 teaspoon salt
1 teaspoon vanilla extract
1 cup buttermilk
2 1/2 cups sifted all-purpose flour
1 1/2 teaspoons baking soda
1 tablespoon distilled white vinegar

Icing:
5 tablespoons all-purpose flour
1 cup milk
1 cup white sugar
1 cup butter, room temperature
1 teaspoon vanilla extract

Directions

1. Preheat the oven* to 350 degrees F (175 degrees C). Grease two 9-inch round pans.
2. Beat the shortening and sugar until very light and fluffy. Add the eggs and beat well.
3. Make a paste of cocoa and red food coloring; add this to the creamed mixture. Mix the salt, vanilla, and buttermilk together. Add the flour to the batter, alternating with the buttermilk mixture. Mix the soda and vinegar and gently fold into the cake batter. Don't beat or stir the batter after this point.
4. Pour the batter into the prepared pans. Bake in the preheated oven until a tester inserted into the cakes comes out clean (about 30 minutes). Cool the cakes completely on a wire rack.
5. To make the icing: Cook the flour and milk on the stove* over low heat until the mixture is thick, stirring constantly. Turn off the heat and let it cool completely! While the mixture is cooling, beat the sugar, butter, and vanilla together until they're light and fluffy. Add the cooled flour mixture and beat until the frosting can be spread. Frost the cake layers when they're completely cool.

Have an adult help you operate the oven and stove.

29

GLOSSARY

abolitionist (ab-uh-LISH-un-ist)—someone who worked to end slavery

amendment (uh-MEND-ment)—a change to a legal document

civil rights (SIV-ull RYTSS)—rights for equal opportunity regardless of race or religion

colonies (KOLL-uh-neez)—lands with ties to a mother country

commemorate (kuh-MEM-uh-rayt)—remember

Confederacy (kun-FED-ur-uh-see)—the group of 11 southern states that tried to leave the United States, causing the Civil War (1860–1865)

Emancipation Proclamation (ee-man-sih-PAY-shun prok-luh-MAY-shun)—document that declared that all enslaved people were free

enslaved (en-SLAYVD)—a person who is forced to work without pay for someone else

plantation (plan-TAY-shun)—a large farm where crops are grown

symbol (SIM-bull)—an object, image, or word that stands for an idea

Union (YOON-yun)—the group of northern states that did not support slavery during the Civil War

LEARN MORE

BOOKS

Duncan, Alice Faye. *Opal Lee and What It Means to Be Free: The True Story of the Grandmother of Juneteenth*. New York, NY: HarperCollins, 2022.

Johnson, Angela. *All Different Now: Juneteenth, the First Day of Freedom*. New York, NY: Simon & Schuster Books for Young Readers, 2014.

Weatherford, Carole Boston. *Juneteenth Jamboree*. New York, NY: Lee & Low, 2008.

Wesley, Valerie. *Freedom's Gifts: A Juneteenth Story*. New York, NY: Simon & Schuster Books for Young Readers, 1997.

WEBSITES

Visit our website for links about Juneteenth and other holidays:
childsworld.com/links

Note to Parents, Teachers, and Librarians: We routinely verify our Web links to make sure they are safe and active sites. So encourage your readers to check them out!

INDEX